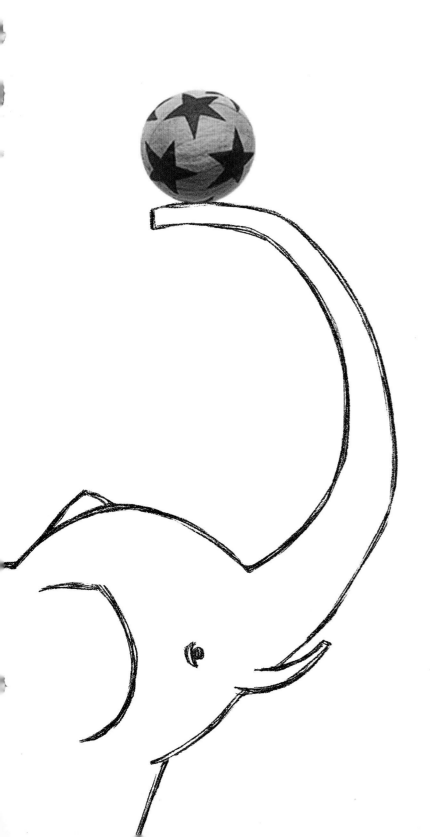

For Nancy and the exceptional hand papermakers in Japan

Text and illustrations copyright © 2014 by Cybèle Young

Published in Canada by Tundra Books, a division of Random House of Canada Limited,
One Toronto Street, Suite 300, Toronto, Ontario M5C 2V6

Published in the United States by Tundra Books of Northern New York,
P.O. Box 1030, Plattsburgh, New York 12901

Library of Congress Control Number: 2013943888

LIBRARY AND ARCHIVES CANADA CATALOGUING IN PUBLICATION

Young, Cybèle, 1972-, author, illustrator
Nancy knows / written and illustrated by Cybèle Young.

Issued in print and electronic formats.
ISBN 978-1-77049-482-4 (bound).—ISBN 978-1-77049-483-1 (epub)

I. Title.

PS8647.O622N35 2014   jC813'.6   C2013-904483-3
                                           C2013-904484-1

Edited by Tara Walker
The artwork in this book was rendered in graphite pencil and sculptures made with Japanese papers.
The text was set in Filosofia.

www.tundrabooks.com

Printed and bound in China

1 2 3 4 5 6   19 18 17 16 15 14

NANCY KNOWS

cybèle young

TUNDRA BOOKS

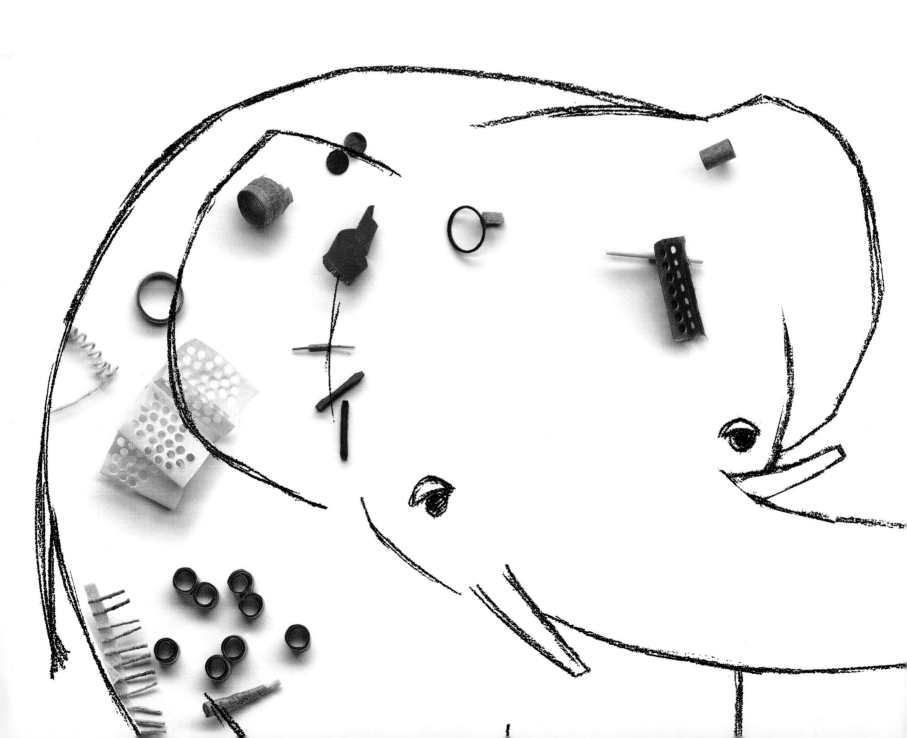

Nancy knows she's forgotten something.
Something important . . .

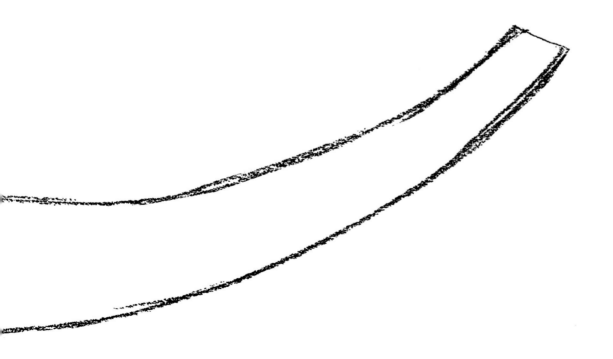

Often when Nancy tries to remember,

she thinks of all kinds of other things.

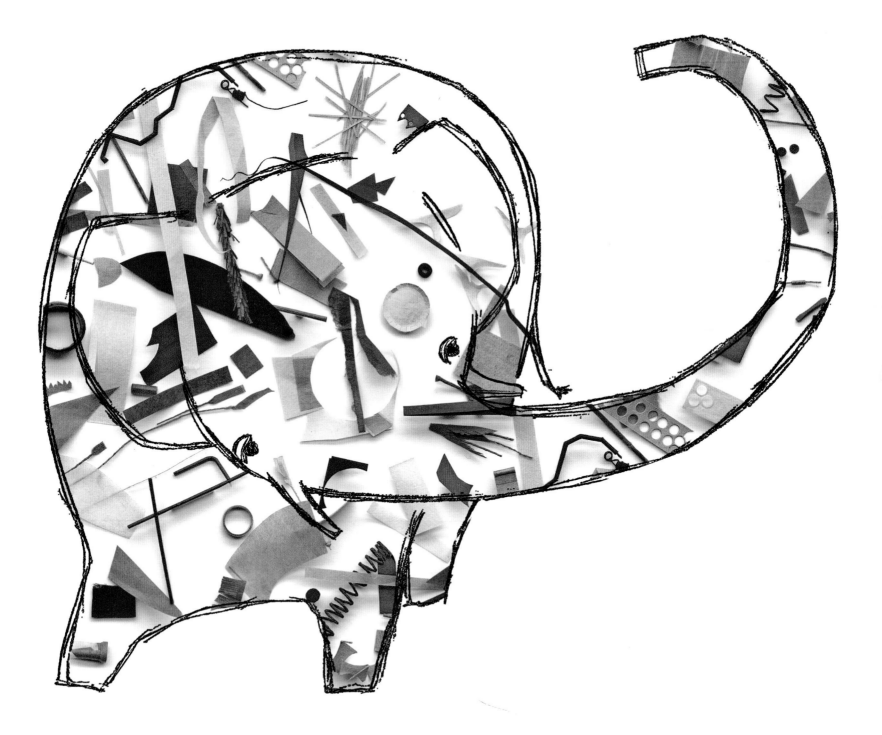

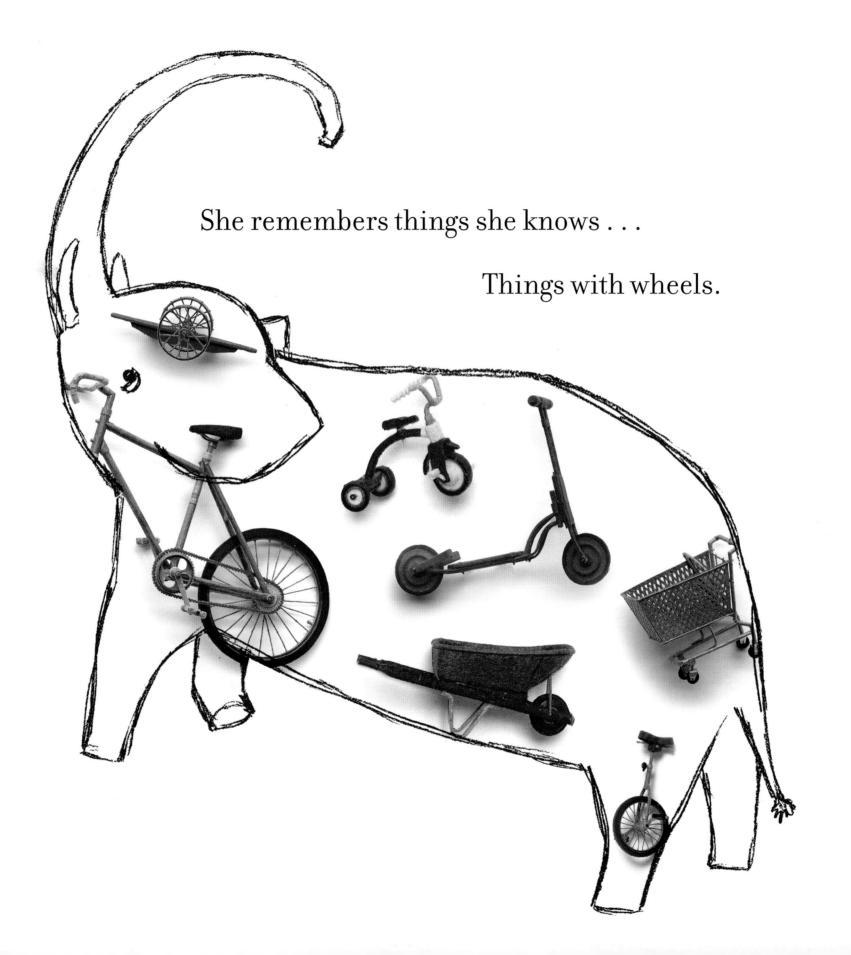

She remembers things she knows . . .

Things with wheels.

Things like clothes.

Places to relax.

And places to go.

She remembers things she doesn't quite know . . .

Things all the same color.

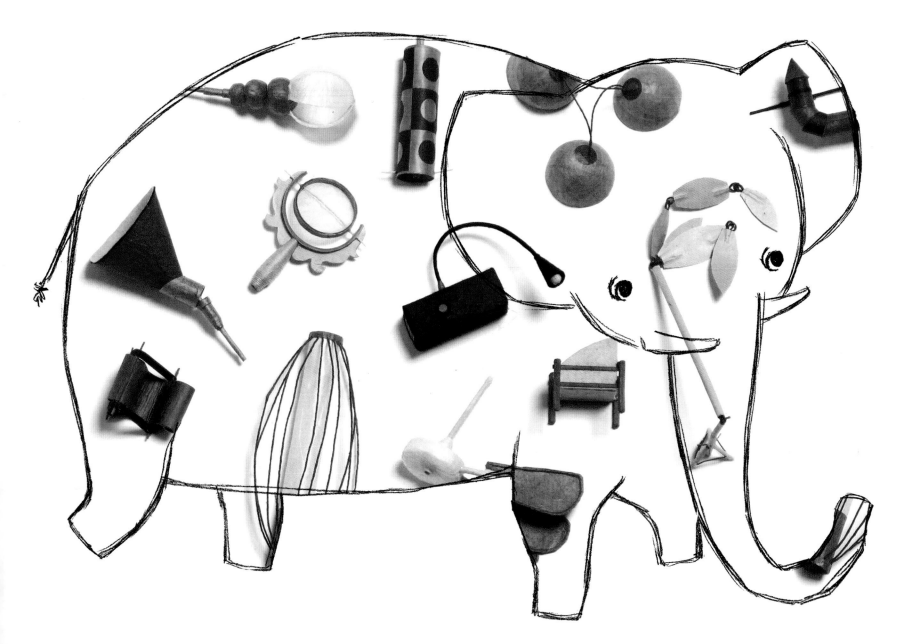

Or all the same shape.

She remembers things one way.

Then another.

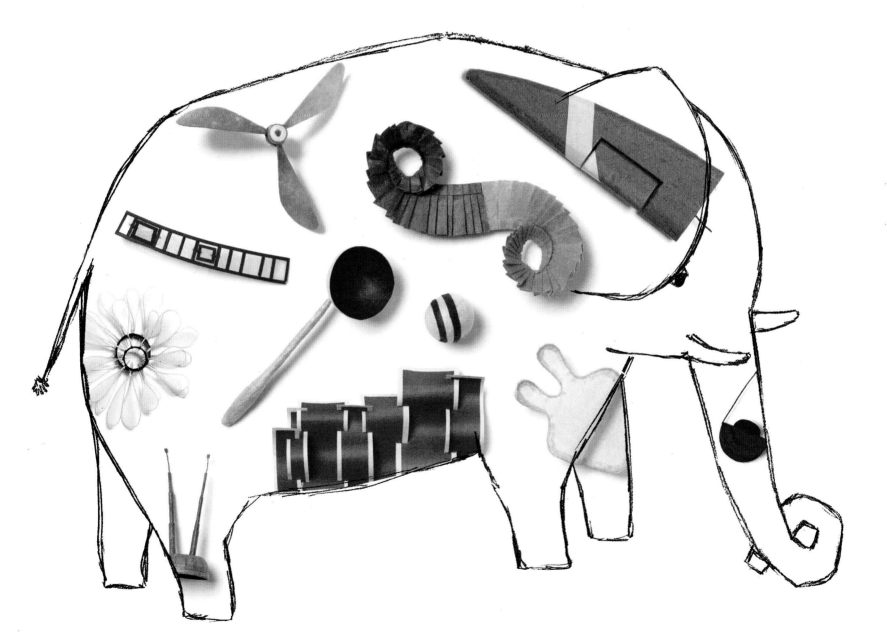

Backwards.

And forwards.

All in neat rows.

Or in a jumbled-up mess.

She remembers things from long ago.

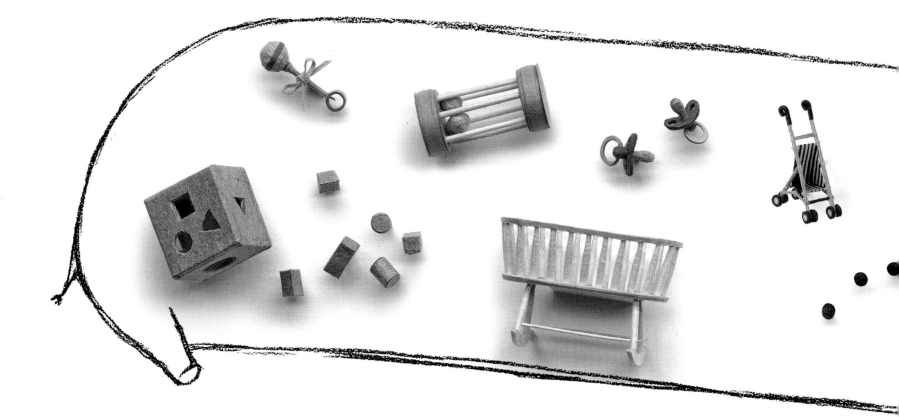

Or two days before tomorrow.

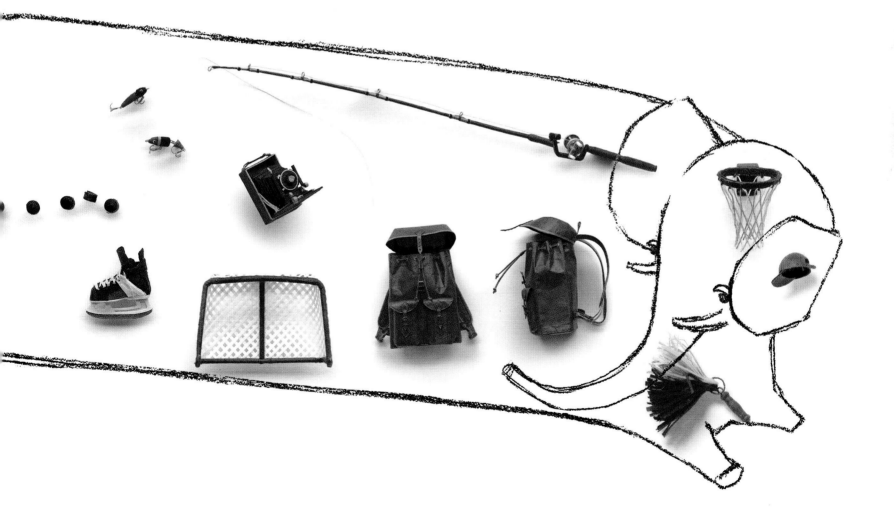

Floating-around things,
just out of reach.
And those that take flight,
then land on the beach.

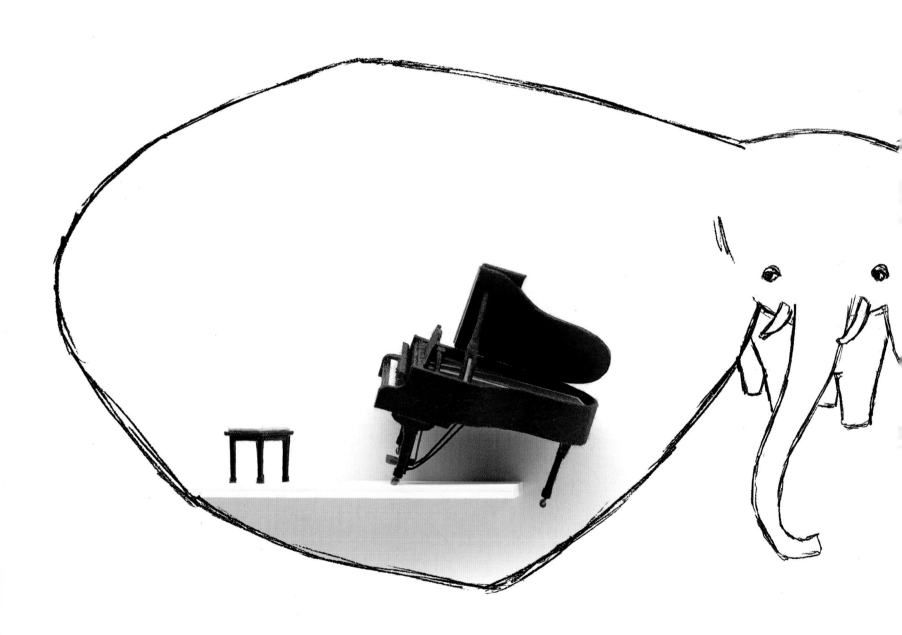

Sometimes Nancy's ears do the remembering.

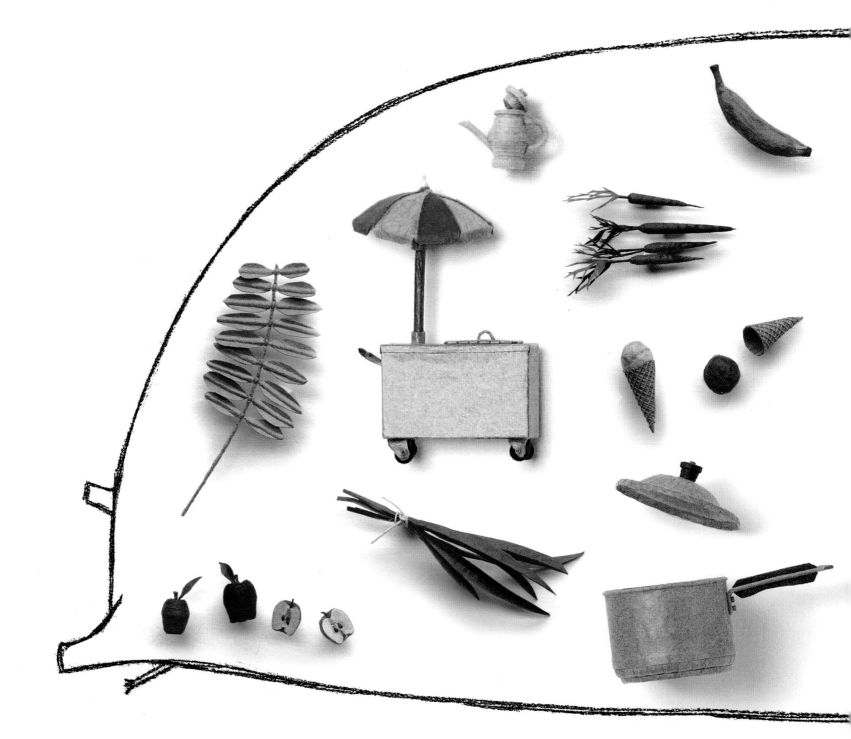

Sometimes her stomach or nose does the work.

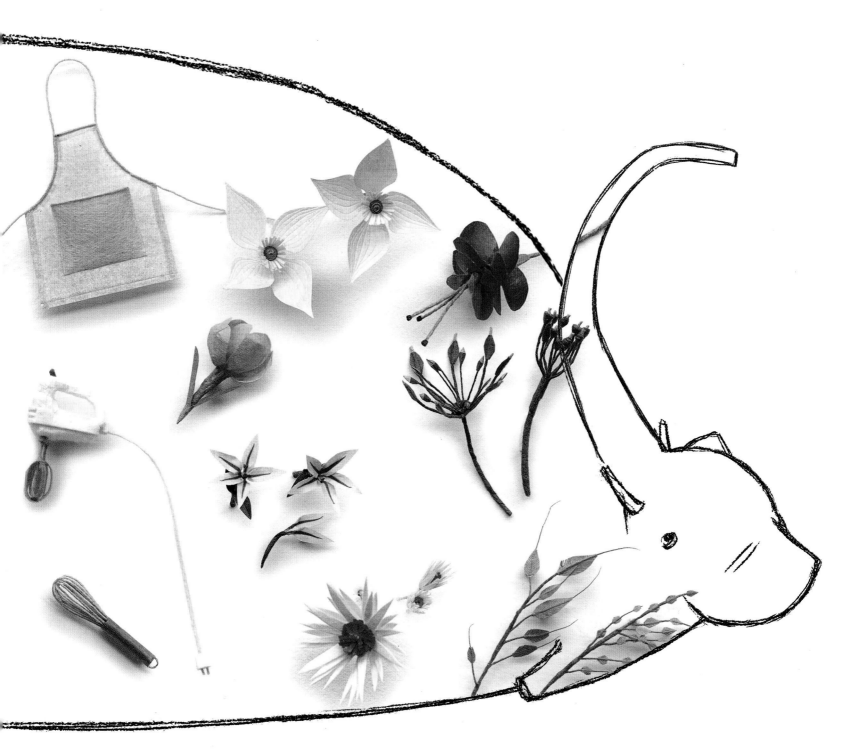

And her heart remembers things from all different places,

all kinds of times and all sorts of spaces.

But Nancy still knows she's forgotten something.

Something important . . .

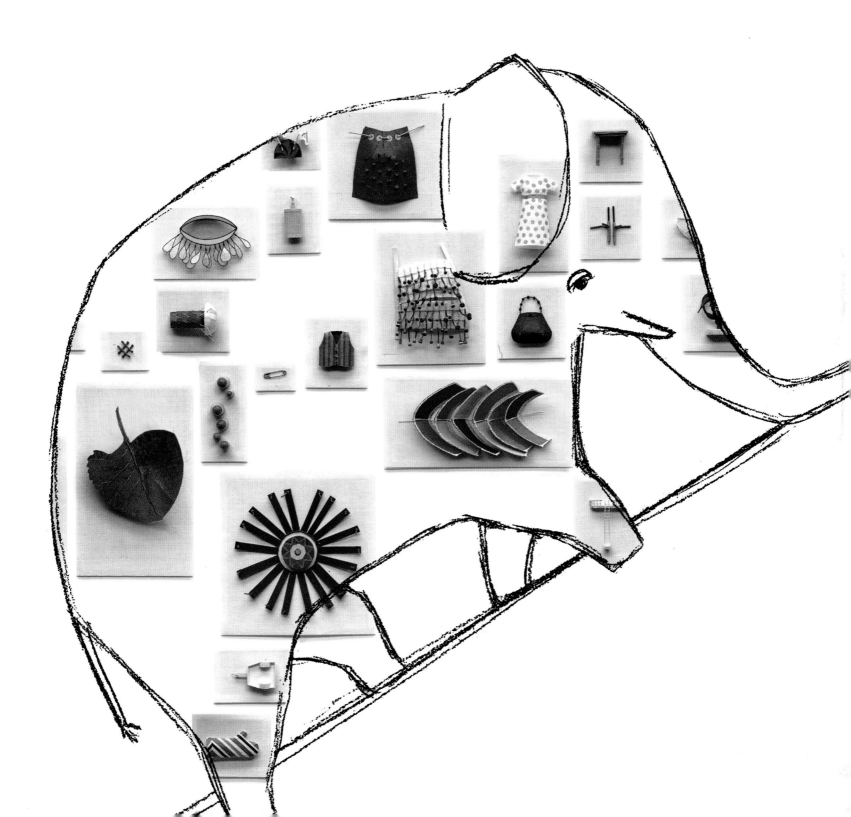

Tired of trying to remember,

Nancy stops thinking altogether.

And that's when she remembers!

"Oscar's waiting for me at the park!"